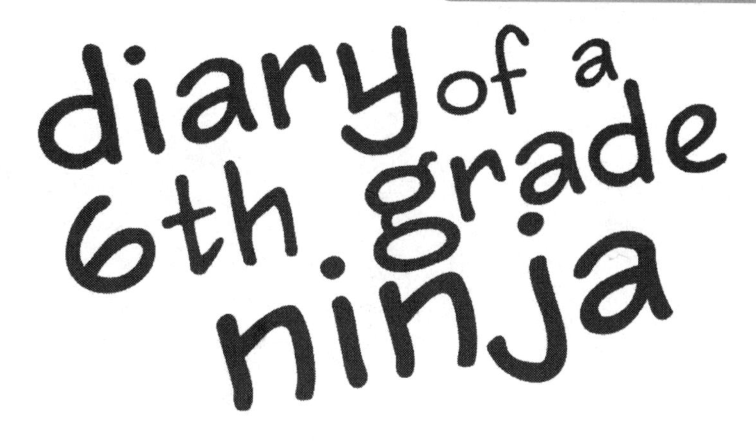

BY MARCUS EMERSON
AND NOAH CHILD,
WITH SAL HUNTER

ILLUSTRATED BY DAVID LEE

EMERSON PUBLISHING HOUSE

Emerson Publishing House

Book design by Marcus Emerson.

For my kids...

Oh, the life of being a ninja. I know what you're thinking – it's an awesome life filled with secrets, crazy ninja moves, and running on the tops of trees. Well, you're right. I'm not gonna lie to you – it's an absolutely *fantastic* life.

But it wasn't always that way.

This might surprise you, but ninjas are often seen as the *bad* guys. I know, right? I had no idea either until I became one. Though looking back, I should've seen the signs early on. You know what they say – hindsight is 20/20.

So this is my story – my diary…er, my *chronicle*. I feel as though it has to be told for others to read so they can learn about the events at Buchanan School. History has to be studied and learned from or else it's destined to repeat itself. And that's something I cannot allow.

My name is Chase Cooper, and I'm eleven years old.

I'm the kind of kid that likes to read comic books and watch old horror movies with my dad. If you were to see me walking down the street, you'd try your best not to bump into me, but only because I'm sorta scrawny. I see all these articles online with titles about losing weight and getting rid of unwanted body fat, and my jaw just drops because I can't gain weight to save my life! I've started working out with my dad when he gets home from work, but it's hard to keep up with him.

All this to say that if you saw me, the last thing you'd think was "dangerous ninja."

I'm not the most popular kid in school, that's for sure. I've never had a girlfriend, and I've never played sports outside of gym class. That's not true – I was on a soccer team in third grade, but after a shin guard to the face and a broken nose, I quit.

So I'm scrawny and unpopular. What else can I apply to those two traits for a completely wretched experience? The *start* of school. But wait! Let's multiply that by a million – I'm also the *new* kid at this particular school.

My parents decided to move across town over the summer so we could live in a slightly larger house. I mean, really? How selfish is *that*? A bigger house, but social death for me! Being in a new district means an entire herd of new students that I don't know.

Well, that's not entirely true either. I know Zoe. She's the same age as me, but doesn't really count because she's my cousin.

Luckily, we had the same gym class together. She was surprised to see me on that first day. I remember it well – it was a Monday, and the day I caught my first glimpse of the ninjas at Buchanan.

"Chase?" Zoe asked. She was wearing gym shorts and a tank top with the school's mascot on it.

"Hey, Zoe," I said.

She looked surprised. "It *is* you! What're you doing *here*?"

Going to school, dummy. That's what I *wanted* to say, but decided against it. "My parents moved to this side of town so I go to school here now."

Zoe laughed. "That's so cool! My own cousin in the same school as me! What fun we'll have!"

I looked at her silky hair and perfect skin. She kind of looked like one of those models on teenybopper magazines. Yeah, there was no way she'd keep herself affiliated with the likes of me, but I gave her the benefit of the doubt. "Uh-huh, it'll be great," I sighed.

The coach, Mr. Cooper, was at the front of the gymnasium checking off students he knew. He walked up

to the rest and asked for their names and grade. Finally, he approached Zoe and me.

"Good morning, Zoe," Mr. Cooper said as he scraped a checkmark into the attendance list. Then he looked at me. "And what's your name?"

Zoe answered for me. "This is Chase Cooper. He's my cousin," she said with a smile.

"Good to have you here," said Mr. Cooper. Then he pointed at Zoe. "She's a good kid to have as a cousin. It's the start of school, but I've already seen her on several try-out lists. You'll do good to follow her lead."

I faked a smile. "Sure."

As Mr. Cooper walked away, Zoe continued speaking. "Why didn't you tell me you were starting at this school?"

I shrugged my shoulders. "We don't really talk that much, and it never came up in conversation. We hardly ever see each other."

Zoe crinkled her nose. "We see each other *every weekend*. Our families have Sunday brunch together at the park!"

I couldn't argue with her. "It's just a little embarrassing."

"You have nothing to be embarrassed about. Starting a new school might be weird, but it's not like you have the ability to control a situation like that," she said.

I didn't want to tell her I was embarrassed and scared of being the new kid. That making friends isn't a strength of mine, and I'm destined to be that kid who walks swiftly through the hallways, clutching my backpack straps and staring at the floor, hoping I don't make eye contact with someone with anger management issues. So I didn't say any of that. "You're right. I think it's just the first day jitters, y'know?"

Zoe's eyes sparkled. She didn't have a clue. "Welcome to the club. We've *all* got the first day jitters. My dad always says the pool is coldest when you first touch the water so the best thing to do is dive right in."

I wasn't sure what my cousin was trying to say. So I replied with, "Wise words."

Zoe looked off to her left and noticed a boy standing alone. "That's Wyatt. He's never really talked to anyone here. He keeps to himself – always has. Which is why he probably doesn't have any friends."

Wyatt was short. He had wavy black hair and a pale complexion that would make a vampire jealous. He kind of looked like a porcelain doll. "Has anyone tried to be *his* friend?"

"Actually, yes. *I* tried talking to him last year, but he wouldn't hear any of it," she sighed. "He was a *jerk* to me."

"Why are you telling me this?" I asked.

Zoe glanced at me. "Because I don't want you to be like him."

I tightened a smile. When I looked back at Wyatt, he was gone.

"So have you raised any money yet for the food drive?" Zoe asked out of nowhere.

"Food drive?" I asked. "I haven't heard of anything about that."

"They sent a pamphlet to all of the student's houses last week," she said. "Oh, that's right… you just moved into your new place, didn't you?"

I nodded.

"Well, it's probably somewhere at your house. We're supposed to raise money by selling fruit or something. I'm already up to ten boxes sold."

"Is there a prize or anything?" I asked. Normally these kinds of things had cool prizes – ray guns and little helicopters and stuff.

"Not a prize for one person, but if the school collectively raises over ten grand, we get to take a trip the week before school is out."

"Where to?"

Zoe shrugged her shoulders. "Does it matter? Anything to get out of school for a day."

I smiled at my cousin. She was actually a little cooler than I thought.

Mr. Cooper opened the side door to the gymnasium. Thank goodness too because Zoe's conversation was making me feel a little edgy. He stepped outside and held the door open with his foot, ushering the rest of us to exit the gym for some "productive activity" outside. Great, just what I needed. Exercise.

Outside, the students were given a few different options. Being the first day of school, Mr. Cooper apparently thought the best thing to do was take it lightly and allow kids to choose what sport they wanted to play. Some played football. Only a couple played basketball. The rest of them, like me, chose to walk laps around the track. It was the easiest option that didn't require choosing teams or working up a sweat.

I could tell Zoe wanted to play football with a few of her friends, but decided to walk the track by my side. It wasn't a huge sacrifice for her, but I appreciated it. A little goes a long way with me.

"So what do you want to know?" she asked.

I didn't understand her question. "What do you mean?"

"About this school. What do you want to know about this school? I imagine most schools are the same, but there's gotta be a *couple* differences here and there. What'd you do at your old school?"

I thought about it for a moment. "I didn't do much. I was in the art club, but that's about it."

"That's fun," Zoe said as she started skipping along the track.

Zoe reminded me of my sister, Lucy, who was also somewhere in the building, adjusting to life as a new student. To be fair, it was far easier for her since she was in third grade. Most third graders barely even know they exist. They haven't become "self aware" yet – like artificial intelligence that hasn't realized it has an identity.

Zoe spoke in an excited manner, which was surprisingly contagious. "There's a *ton* of stuff to do here. Not a lot of schools have as much as us. Buchanan actually prides itself on how huge of a selection we have. There's all kinds of sports teams, different groups, and a bunch of random clubs you can join. I'm sure there's an art club somewhere around here. I'll help you find it."

I nodded my head, but was distracted by some movement out of the corner of my eye. It was the edge of the track where the tree line was the thickest. I stopped in place and stared for a second to see if anything moved again, but nothing did.

"What is it?" Zoe asked.

I kept staring into the dense foliage. It was just a mess of green leaves and heavy shadows - except for a pair of the whitest eyes I'd ever seen. I froze in place and rubbed my eyes. Am I seeing things straight or was it part of the "first day jitters" that Zoe and I spoke about?

When I looked again, they were gone.

"I guess I just..." I stopped talking when I looked at Zoe's face.

Zoe was standing behind me with her eyes peeled wide open, staring into the same spot in the tree line that I was studying only seconds ago. "Did you see that?" she asked.

A chill ran down my spine. "I did. Do you know what it was?"

She shook her head and started walking along the track again. "Come on. Let's get out of here. I think I'd rather *not* get eaten by a creature in the woods today."

I knew it wasn't a monster that we had seen. I'm not that into scary stories and watch enough with my dad to know that monsters are fake… at least I *think* they're fake. At that moment, I didn't feel the need to test that theory so I caught up with Zoe and we spent the rest of class making jokes to distract ourselves from whatever it was that had spied on us.

Little did I know that it was the first time I'd ever seen a ninja. I'd do anything to take that moment back and just keep walking. Of course, that's not how it turned out, and my curiosity got the better of me.

Tuesday. 10:30 AM. Gym class.

The next day, Mr. Cooper took attendance as he did before. I was surprised that he remembered who I was. As he approached me, he said my name and checked me off the list.

Zoe hadn't left the girl's locker room yet so I was stuck in the gymnasium standing by myself. I pushed my hands into my pockets and watched the other kids laugh and make jokes with each other before the class officially started. A couple of them even glanced in my direction. I didn't hear what they said, but I'm pretty sure it was about me.

"Hey, *new* kid," said a voice from behind me.

I turned around and was met by a taller student. He was very plain looking with slicked back brown hair. It's possible that it was greasy, but it's also possible he just used way too much gel. "Me?" I asked.

The brown haired boy outstretched his arms. "I don't see any other *new* kids around here, do you?"

I glanced around. "Uh, I guess I wouldn't know."

"Of course not," he said as he held out his hand. "My name's Brayden, and *you* just passed my *test*."

I shook his cold clammy hand. It was gross and I had to very consciously decide not to rip my hand away from his in disgust. It was my second day of school! I didn't want to embarrass anyone… *yet*. "My name's Chase. Chase Cooper. What test did I just pass?"

Brayden shrugged his shoulders. "I don't know. It's just an icebreaker. Y'know, something to break… the *ice*."

Smart one, this kid. "Nice to meet you."

"Pleased to meet *you*, Chase. So how was your first day of class yesterday?"

"It was alright," I answered. As I blinked, I hoped he couldn't read my thoughts. Please just walk away. You're weird and sweaty.

"Huh," Brayden grunted as he crossed his arms. He remained in place like a statue.

What did this kid want me to say? That it was an epic first day? That it was lame? Whatever it was, I guess I didn't care because I didn't try to keep the conversation going. We stood there in an awkward silence, occasionally making eye contact, wondering who the next to speak would be.

"Chase," Zoe called from nearby. "Come on, let's walk the track again."

I glanced at Brayden. He still didn't say anything. He just stood there looking sad. Being the nice guy I am, I couldn't just walk away from him. "You want to join us?"

Brayden's face slowly cracked open a smile. It was one of the scariest things I'd seen in my life. "Sure!" he said.

Zoe was nice about it. She seemed to know Brayden from previous years at this school. "Hi, Brayden. Find any werewolves lately?"

"No, but it's not for lack of trying," Brayden answered.

Suddenly, Brayden seemed a little more interesting to me. "You look for werewolves?"

"*Hunt* werewolves," he said sharply. "I *hunt* werewolves."

Yeah, this kid was cool. "Ever find any?" I asked.

"Never," he replied. "Not a one."

"Maybe someday," I said. It was pretty unlikely that this dude was going to catch a werewolf, but who was I to shatter his dreams? "Just keep trying I guess."

As we stepped out of the gym doors, the sun poured across the school parking lot like a hot wet blanket. It was muggy and awful outside. Zoe immediately started flapping the bottom of her tank top to push air through the shirt.

"Oh gross," she said. "Great. Everyone's gonna sweat and stink for the rest of the day. That's so nasty."

I laughed. When she said it like that, it *did* seem nasty. Zoe was always the cleanest one at family events, always washing her hands and wiping her face.

As we walked the path to the track, Brayden was talking about his love of werewolves. At first it was great, but it got boring really fast. He just kept repeating the same things over and over about how real werewolves live in Wisconsin or something. This boy would *not* shut his mouth.

Zoe was good at pretending to care though I know she actually didn't. Seeing her smile and nod, I realized how obvious it actually was and wondered if she had ever done that to me. Didn't matter – we hardly talked outside of school.

"So that's why a lot of people think werewolves

actually come from *Wisconsin*," Brayden said, breathing heavily.

"That's *neat*!" Zoe said, almost convincingly.

"What happens if you ever find one?" I asked.

Brayden paused. "Of course I want to find one someday, but at the same time, I hope I never do. If I ever get close enough to one, I'll probably snap a picture with my camera. That is, if I have my camera on me."

Zoe started glancing at the tree line again as soon as we arrived to the track. There were several other students in front of us with even more trailing behind. I knew she was looking for those eyes from yesterday. What could they have possible been? And then I glanced at Brayden…

"Hey," I said to him. "Have you ever heard any stories of anything living in *these* woods?"

Zoe's attention snapped at me. Her brow was furrowed and if she could stare daggers into my soul, she totally would have.

"In *these* woods?" Brayden asked as he looked at the trees. "I've never heard anything strange about them. Why? Did you see something?"

Zoe's glare warned me not to mention anything, but she's family – she'll forgive me. "I saw a set of eyes watching me yesterday. Zoe saw them too."

"*Why* would you say anything?" Zoe asked. She looked at Brayden. "If you tell *anyone* about this, just say it was *Chase* that saw something, okay? I don't need this kind of paranoid delusion following me into middle school next year."

Brayden scratched his head. "You two saw someone watching you from the trees? What color were the eyes?"

"Blue," I answered. At least I *remembered* them being blue.

Brayden scratched at his rough chin. "Y'know… I've heard stories… no. There's no way."

Suddenly Zoe was interested. All this "cool girl" talk disappears when you put a real mystery in front of her face. "There's no way, what? What were you *going* to say?"

Brayden stepped closer to the tree line. Naturally, Zoe and I followed. As he leaned into the shadows, he mumbled some stuff to himself, but I couldn't understand what he was saying. It was strange… it sounded as if he said… *ninjas*.

And then he reached his hand into the woods. I knew what was about to happen next because it happens in movies all the time. The innocent doofus reaches his hand into a dark area and loses it.

"Wait!" I shouted, but it was too late.

Brayden was suddenly yanked into the trees. In a rush of activity, he disappeared. It looked as if shadows came to life and swallowed him up. I just met this kid and I already regretted it.

Zoe cupped her hand over her mouth, muffling a scream I knew would come out sooner or later. Without thinking (I seem to be guilty of this a lot), I jumped into the woods to chase after Brayden.

"No!" I could hear Zoe yell.

As soon as I planted my feet into the ground beyond the border of the woods, I kept my eyes clenched tight, afraid of what kind of monsters I would be face to face with. Was Brayden's theory of werewolves correct? Was one going to be standing there with a half eaten boy in its jaws? I forced my eyes open.

Nothing.

The area was empty. There were no monsters, no people, and no Brayden. I scanned farther through the trees, focusing on seeing any kind of movement against the still areas, but there was nothing.

In that moment, the branches shook from behind me. I thought my heart was going to explode as I flipped around to face my attacker. In all the chaos, I forgot that

Zoe was even with me. Weird too because less than ten seconds had passed since I jumped into the woods.

"Where's Brayden?" Zoe whispered.

"I don't know," I answered. "And I can't even tell where they took him!"

"Who's '*they*'?"

I shrugged my shoulders. "Werewolves, I guess? Maybe they've finally gotten fed up with his terrible hunting skills and have taken action into their own paws. Get it? Paws?" It was a terrible joke, but hopefully it helped Zoe feel better.

She laughed. "Human hunters," she sneered. "Too bad they picked the strangest kid to kidnap and study, right? Look at the ground."

I did, but couldn't see what she was talking about. It was just moist dirt, or *mud* as a scientist would probably call it. "What about it?"

"There's no tracks," Zoe said. "It doesn't even look like there are tracks from *Brayden.* Whatever yanked him in here *had* to have struggled with him, right?"

"Yeah," I said. "I don't think Brayden would've gone willingly. And there wouldn't have been enough time to cover any tracks because I followed him in here almost immediately."

"What did you see right after you stepped through the trees?"

Another chill ran down my spine. "*Nothing*. There was *nothing* back here. No signs of anything that would've grabbed him, and even stranger, no sign of Brayden himself."

Zoe folded her arms and made the "smartie-pants" face I hate. "You know what I'm wondering?"

"Do tell," I sighed.

"I'm wondering why we don't just go straight to the coach with this. Why follow Brayden in here? It's counter-productive. Mr. Cooper would probably get the police and Brayden would be found in an instant."

"Unless it was *werewolves*," whispered a voice from above.

My body froze as I stared at my cousin. She was staring right back at me with her eyes as wide as I'd ever seen on a person that *wasn't* a cartoon. For a split second, I wanted to warn her that they'd fall out of her head. She'd probably slap my arm for being hilarious at an inappropriate time.

I looked up in the trees and was surprised by what I saw. *Nothing again.* A whole lot of nothing happening out there today.

"Right here, buck-o," whispered the voice again, this time from in front of Zoe and me.

When I turned, I saw not only one kid standing in front of us, but several. There must've been fifteen or twenty of them, all dressed in the same black uniforms. Their faces were covered with masks that only showed their eyes. There was no way this was happening, right? These kinds of things only happen in movies, and mostly movies from the eighties! My *dad's* movies.

"Are you…" I started asking.

"*Ninjas*," said the child in the mask. The rest of the ninjas behind him punched their chest once and let out a "ha!" sound at the same time. I couldn't help but chuckle at how choreographed it was.

"What's so funny?" asked the ninja. "You *dare* laugh at us?"

"Not at *you*," I said. "Just at the fact that it all sounded like you were gonna laugh at the same time, but stopped instead. Plus you're a bunch of kids out here wearing pajamas and hiding in the woods. If *that's* not a red flag for a guidance counselor, I don't know what is. Besides, you guys aren't very good since you're all standing here in front of us right now. Aren't ninjas supposed to be a secret?"

The ninja stepped forward, revealing Brayden standing behind him. "We've taken your friend prisoner because he got too close to our operation. We've revealed ourselves to *you* because there was a possibility you'd seek help from Mr. Cooper. We've come too far as a clan and can't let it all fizzle out because of a tattle tale."

"Are you alright?" Zoe asked Brayden.

Brayden nodded, but didn't say anything.

The first ninja spoke again. "We'll release him to you under one condition."

What a strange school. I've been here one day and I've already met a clan of secret ninjas that's holding a kid I just met hostage. How valuable was Brayden to me? Not very. I only just met the boy, but again, being the nice guy I am… "Name it."

"You walk out of these woods and tell no one what you saw today," said the ninja.

"But master," said one of the ninjas from the back. I was surprised because it was a girl's voice. "They've seen too much! We cannot let them leave here!"

The first ninja raised his fist in the air. She quickly bowed out of respect and stepped back in line. This kid had power, I'll admit that.

"Fine," I said as I glanced at my cousin.

"Deal," said Zoe.

They released Brayden. He stumbled toward us with his hands behind his back. In the short amount of time they had him, they had already tied his hands together. Maybe they were better than I thought.

At that moment, I heard the air horn Mr. Cooper uses to signal when there was five minutes left of class. It was his way of lazily telling us to return to the gym. Zoe, Brayden, and I turned toward the school.

When I looked back, the ninjas were gone without a trace.

Wednesday. 7:45 AM. Homeroom.

Buchanan School had started sixth graders on a schedule similar to middle school so the transfer in the next year wouldn't be as shocking. It was cool because we were the only kids that had this type of schedule in the school. I guess everyday was going to start with a fifteen-minute homeroom, where we'd all gather our things together and take attendance. Another cool thing about it was no assigned seating. Students were allowed to sit wherever they wanted.

I was the last in the room just before the bell rang.

"Cutting it close, aren't you?" Zoe asked as she unzipped her backpack. It was bright red with speckled straps. There was a small plastic sleeve on the side that had her name written on it. She made a smiley face with the "o."

I smiled and mocked her. "*You're* cutting it close."

"That doesn't even make sense," she replied.

"Think about it for a minute, and it *will*," I said.

Zoe's eyes darted back and forth and the gears in her head clearly cranked. In the time it took her to think, I sat in the seat behind her. Finally she turned around.

"I still don't get it," she said.

Poor Zoe. *That* was the joke, but I didn't have the heart to tell her. "Nevermind."

Homeroom went on as the teacher made the announcements for the day. I zoned out watching the clock as the sound of their voice trailed over my head, speaking about football try-outs, the school lunch menu, and other dumb things that didn't concern me. Something about the food drive and how it was only the third day of school and a quarter of the way to our goal. I should probably find that thing the school mailed to my house.

As I envisioned the teacher's words floating over my head, I started to see myself floating there as well. I drifted over the other students, free from this horrible place called "school." And then I flipped my body over and saw the clouds over my head. They were white and fluffy, like marshmallows. I positioned my legs to point at the floor and zoomed—

"*Hey*," Zoe's voice said, interrupting my awesome daydream. "You comin' or what?"

I had a way of losing track of reality when I daydreamed. If I were in a job interview, I'd probably try to hide that fact when they asked about my weaknesses. And also my allergy to bees. ADHD and bees are my weaknesses.

Zoe was standing over my desk waiting for me. The other students had already left the room. Man, I must've been *completely* out of it.

"Sorry." I stood from my desk and watched a folded sheet of paper fall to the floor. Someone had wedged it under my forearm when I wasn't paying attention.

"A secret admirer?" Zoe asked. "Already? Chase, you move too quickly for your own good."

I gestured to my scrawny body. "What girl *wouldn't* want this?"

Zoe laughed. It made me feel better.

"What's it say?" Zoe asked.

I unfolded the sheet of paper and read the writing.

Chase,

Be at the edge of the woods today at the start of gym class. Bring your cousin. Cookies and soda will be provided.

There was no signature.

"Cookies and soda?" Zoe asked.

Great. I read the note out loud when I didn't mean to. My dad would always make fun of me because I whispered anything I ever read, even if I meant to read it in my head. "Mouth breather," is what he'd call me. It was in good fun, but got annoying sometimes.

"The ninjas want us to return?" Zoe asked. "And

they're offering soda and cookies as bait? Are they serious? Has anything else in the history of traps ever screamed '*trap*' so loudly?"

"It doesn't say it was from the ninjas," I said. "Maybe it's from Brayden."

"The werewolf boy? Yeah, right. Like he'd be smart enough to pull off a trap like this… actually, maybe you *are* right. It's such an obvious scheme that I wouldn't be surprised it *were* him."

Glancing at the clock, I saw that it was only a little after eight in the morning. Gym wasn't for another two and a half hours. Wonderful. I can't stand waiting for the microwave to beep after a *minute*. How was I going to last two and a half *hours*?

Wednesday. 10:40 AM. Gym class.

By this time, my hands were shaking. I had endured two different classes in anticipation for gym. At one point in the morning, I had even worked up a cold sweat. Zoe made fun of me the whole time.

She was right behind me when I entered into the woods again at the same place as the day before. I clenched my jaw as I stepped foot into the moist dirt, or *mud*, waiting to get punched in the face. Luckily that never happened.

Instead, we were met right away by a shorter ninja. He was alone, carrying a zip locked baggie of Oreo cookies and two orange sodas. In my entire life, I can honestly say I never expected a ninja to greet me with cookies and drinks. It was weird.

"What's this about?" I asked.

"You'll see soon enough," the ninja whispered as

he turned around. "Eat your cookies and follow me."

Now I know that I should be cautious when given snacks by a shady character, but c'mon… they were *Oreo cookies*! Did I mention they were *double stuffed*? I think even the best of us have our weaknesses.

"Lead the way," I said, grabbing the baggie of cookies.

"You're seriously going to eat those?" Zoe asked as she followed behind.

"Darn right."

Zoe smirked. "Good. 'Cause I didn't want to be the only one eating them. Gimme some."

I took a cookie from the zip locked bag and handed it to her. The ninja in front of us wasn't walking very

quickly. Maybe he wasn't in as much of a hurry as we were, but gym class was only fifty minutes long, and twenty minutes had already passed.

"Stop," the ninja said. And then he turned around to face us again. "We're here."

Without moving my head, I glanced around the area in front of us. "So we only walked about ten steps, and now we're in your secret hideout? There's no one here. What gives?"

The ninja didn't answer. He slowly lifted his hand up, pointing at something behind us. When I turned around, I saw what he was pointing at.

Zoe and I had only walked about ten feet. We were only about fourteen feet from the edges of the woods that we entered. But in the amount of time it took us to walk this far, the entire clan of ninjas had quietly entered into the area. They stood like charcoal colored statues facing us.

"Man, these guys are *good*," I whispered.

"They're *alright*," Zoe said.

The ninja at the front of the group approached us. I couldn't be sure, but I thought maybe it was the same short one from the day before. As I studied his movement, I kind of thought he looked like a "mini-ninja." Y'know, almost like a toy. This thought caused me to chuckle again.

"What's so funny?" the ninja asked. He even had a higher pitched voice. It *wasn't* the ninja from the day before.

"It's nothing. I just—"

"Do you know why you're here?" the ninja asked, interrupting me.

I pulled the note from my gym shorts. I had been anxious all day about this meeting, which meant that I opened and closed the note about a hundred times, reading and re-reading it. The sheet of paper was falling apart as I held it out to the masked boy. "I got this in homeroom."

The ninja shook his small head. "You're here because we've *allowed* you to be. You've been invited to join our clan. It's not an invitation you should take ligh—"

This time, *I* interrupted him. "*Yes*. Yes, yes, and yes please, with a side of French onion *yes*."

The ninja paused. "You haven't even heard our proposal yet."

"I don't care," I replied. "Ninjas are the coolest thing since wireless video game controllers. Of course I want to be a ninja!"

Zoe folded her arms and grumbled.

The short kid looked at her. "The invitation is for *you* as well, darling."

"Ew," Zoe said. "*Don't* call me darling."

"Apologies," the ninja said. "Your cousin has just decided to join our clan. What says you?"

"Meh," Zoe said. "Is this whole thing a secret?"

The ninja nodded like a bobble-head toy. Seriously, he looked like a stinkin' child's play thing!

“So nobody will ever know I was in this club?” Zoe asked.

“Correct.”

After a sigh, she looked at me and tightened her lips. “Why not? Sounds like fun.”

“Excellent!” shouted the ninja in front of us. The minions behind him all raised their arms in the air and exalted with the same “*ha*” sound as the day before. The ninja turned around, but glanced over his shoulder at us. “Be here tomorrow at this time. If you wish to join our clan, each of you must find a four leafed clover and present it to us in this spot.”

“Wait,” I said. “We’re not automatically entered into your little ninja gang?”

The boy remained silent as he nodded his head. I could tell from his squinty eyes that he was smiling under the mask. And then he spoke loudly. “Ninja *vanish*!”

Immediately, two ninjas hopped down from the treetops and started clapping chalkboard erasers together violently in front of my face. The white powder of chalk exploded into the air, making it impossible to see anything. When the smoke cleared, the ninjas were gone.

“Amazing,” I whispered.

“A little dorky,” Zoe snipped quietly.

“Then why’d you say you’d join?”

Zoe’s shoulders slumped down and she waved her arms out. “Because you’re *new* at this school, and I want you to feel normal about it. I don’t know what it’s like being the new kid, but I’m sure it *stinks*. If joining a ninja clan will help you get on your feet, then by golly, *that's* what I'll do." She paused. "*What a weird sentence I just spoke!* I do it 'cause you're family, y'know. You're cool enough, Chase, but if it takes a little bit of a push, then *I'll* be the one to push."

I smiled at the sappy way she was telling me she cared. "Gross, stop it already. You're gonna bore me to the point of comatose."

Zoe shook her head, confused. "That's not even a *thing*!"

Thursday. 7:45 AM. Homeroom.

I took my seat behind Zoe again since the desk was open. She turned around immediately, wearing a stupid grin. I knew why she was grinning and I couldn't help but return the dorky smile.

"Did you find one?" Zoe whispered.

I shook my head. "No. I looked all night in my yard. There were a billion three leafed clovers, and a couple of two leafed ones… even found a *five* leafed clover, but no four leafs. I'll have to spend the first half of gym class with my face buried in the grass looking for one I guess."

She slammed a textbook down on my desk. It made enough ruckus that the entire class noticed.

"Sorry," she said, embarrassed.

"It's alright," said the homeroom teacher as he continued making the announcements. "And the food drive total is up to over three *thousand* dollars! All the cash and checks are sitting in the front office inside a plastic container for everyone to see. It's quite a spectacle, really. If we can fill two of those containers, we'll have made our goal of reaching ten thousand dollars! And you know what *that* means…"

"*Class trip!*" the students said in unison.

When the teacher started speaking again, Zoe turned around and opened the textbook to a page in the middle. At the center of the page were *two* four leafed clovers.

I was shocked. I had a stinkin' magnifying glass when I searched for over three hours the night before! "How'd you find *two* of them?"

"I found them *years* ago," she whispered. "I've always had them."

"Well, when you show them you have two, they'll probably promote you immediately."

Her jaw dropped and she gasped. "Are you *stupid*?

One is for *you*! I brought it in case you couldn't find any!"

Obviously I hoped that was the case, but I didn't want to be rude and *assume* it. I took it from the textbook and studied it closely. "Really? That's… *awesome*. Thanks!"

"Best cousin ever, right?"

I chuckled.

"You guys are seriously considering joining those ninjas?" Brayden's voice asked.

He was in the seat next to us. Strange that I didn't even notice him until he spoke. Guess he had that kind of a personality.

"Why not?" I asked.

"Because they're ninjas. Ninjas *aren't* good guys," Brayden said, slouching in his seat.

"What're you talkin' about?" I said. Is Brayden really against the whole ninja thing? This from a boy who hunts werewolves and brags about it? "Ninjas are all about honor and helping people. I read all about it on the internet last night," I said, which was true. Sad, isn't it?

And I learned some crazy things! Did you know ninjas were mostly peaceful farmers that lived in the mountains? The reason they're all stealthy is so they can defend themselves when they were outnumbered. A few people bought into the fighting system of ninjitsu and went around assassinating people with their skills. And you know what they say – a few bad apples spoil the bunch.

"No," Brayden said. "*Real* ninjas weren't bad guys by default, but the ninjas *you're* talking about joining… *are*."

I shook my head and said the only thing that came to mind. "*Nuh-uh*."

Thursday. 10:35 AM. Gym class.

Zoe and I sprinted toward the wooded area on the track as soon as we exited the gymnasium doors. Mr. Cooper had his sunglasses on and was lying back in a reclining lawn chair just to the right of the exit. His air horn was sitting on the ground next to him. It was the fourth day I've been in this school, and this was the position I was used to seeing him in. Lazy and uncaring. I think I'll be a gym teacher when I get older.

Once we entered the trees, the ninjas were there waiting for us. I guess there wasn't any reason to sneak up or anything since we had an appointment.

The shortest of the ninjas stepped forward. "I assume you both have your clovers, otherwise it would be pea-brained of you to return here."

At the same time, Zoe and I held out our four leafed clovers.

"Excellent," said the ninja. "*Eat* them."

Did he just say what I think he said? Was this kid crazy? But when I looked at Zoe, she was already chewing on hers. There was no way I'd be shown up by my cousin so I popped the thing into my mouth and started going to town on it. At first, I expected the taste of dirt and grass, but was actually surprised. It wasn't half bad! It was sort of tart and bitter. It's possible that I'd even try it again someday.

"Sick!" the ninja said with a laugh. "I can't believe you guys did that!"

Zoe stopped chewing and looked angry. She spit out the clover and stepped toward the small ninja. "I'm about to make you eat a mouthful of grass, you little—"

The ninja put his hands up, chuckling. "Wait, wait! I'm sorry. It's cool, you guys are in the clan. Seriously, you're *in*."

Zoe perked up. "Really? Because you just made me *eat* a clover."

I don't know why Zoe minded. I was still chewing on mine. "So we're in?"

The ninja pulled the black mask off his face. I gulped the clover down as soon as I recognized the kid – it was Wyatt, the short guy we saw standing alone the other day.

"Wyatt?" Zoe asked. "*You're* the ninja leader?"

"I am," he said nodding. "And the two of you are our newest recruits."

I almost jumped with joy, but I'm not so sure a ninja would hop up and down when they were happy. "*Nice*," I said. "So what's next?"

Wyatt walked past us. The other ninjas remained in place in the woods, watching as he neared the edge and continued speaking. "Now there's just *one* more test to pass."

"But you just said we were in," Zoe grunted with her arms folded. "*In* is *in*, isn't it?"

"Sorta," Wyatt said as he parted some leaves. "But you have to show your allegiance to the clan so that we know you're dead serious."

Oh no. This is what I feared. He was going to have us *kill* someone.

"You must perform a final task," Wyatt said,

studying the other students walking the track on the outside of the woods. "One that's *incriminating*."

"I don't think I can kill anyone," I whispered.

Wyatt looked over his shoulder at me. "Are you *nuts*? *Kill* someone? What's the matter with you?"

I stared at the ground, embarrassed of opening my big mouth. As I kicked at the dirt, I whispered, "It was a joke."

Wyatt shook his head in disbelief. "*Doubt* it," he said as he returned his attention to the innocent bystanders walking the track. "There's no killing here. Come on, *we're sixth graders*."

"Then what is it?" Zoe asked.

Wyatt pointed his finger at one of the girls on the track. She was walking with her friends. A purple and pink purse was slung from her shoulder. "Steal Emily's purse and return it to me within the hour."

Zoe joined Wyatt at his side. "*What*? You want us to steal Emily's purse? Are *you* nuts? We're not stealing anything from anyone! Besides, those girls are my friends!"

Wyatt turned around and looked at me. "Then the two of you are dismissed. Leave this place at once."

I sighed, looking at my cousin. She was standing with her hands on her hips – the usual "you've got to be kidding me" look in her eyes. It's a look I'm familiar with. I didn't want to argue with her, so I didn't, but she must've seen my hesitation.

"Fine," she said softly. She was doing it for me.

"Excellent," said Wyatt as he slipped his mask back on.

"So where's our black pajamas that we wear since we're ninjas?" I asked.

Wyatt shook his head and spoke from behind the fabric on his face. "You get those *after* you return with the purse."

"After?" Zoe asked.

This was going to be more difficult than I thought.

Wyatt and the clan disappeared from behind us. Zoe and I waited until Emily and her friends made a full lap around the track so they were right in front of us again. I could see her purple purse swinging gently over her shoulder. The strap was short. It wouldn't be as easy as sneaking it off her arm.

"What do you think?" I asked Zoe.

"I think I'm gonna be sick," she replied.

She can be such a drama queen. "Thank you for going along with this."

She rolled her eyes. "Pretty sure I'm already regretting it."

I straightened my posture, feeling guilty about Zoe's involvement. I started to talk, to tell her she could back out of it if she wanted, but she interrupted me.

"Look!" she cried as she pointed. "They're taking a break in the grass! She put her purse on the ground!"

When I looked out, I saw that Zoe was right. Emily was laying on her back along with her friends. They were staring at the clouds or something, I couldn't tell exactly what they were doing, but I didn't care. The purse was free from her shoulder.

"Follow my lead," Zoe said as she burst through the tree line.

I jumped through, trying to keep up, but she was fast! She sprinted like some kind of gazelle running from a predator! What was she going to do? Was she just going to snatch the purse and run like heck? I'm pretty sure those girls would notice something as obvious as that and, wait a second. Was she going to use *me* as a distraction?

My heart started to race as I saw the whole disaster play out in my head. She would scrape the purse off the ground. Just as the girls would notice, I'd suddenly appear, hobbling like a penguin because I suck at running. In all the chaos, they would see me as the bad guy and since I'm pretty slow, *I'd* be the one those lions

would devour. *How could Zoe do such a thing to me*?

I watched as my cousin finally made it to her group of friends. My heart stopped as I waited for her to grab the purse, but to my surprise, she didn't. Instead, she tripped just as she reached the circle and tumbled across the grass violently until finally flopping about ten feet away from them.

And then I realized her brilliance. Zoe's friends dashed to her aid as she clutched at her scraped knees. They were so concerned with her that they left all their belongings behind in the grass. There were shoes with socks stuffed into them, stretchy hair bands, and one lonely purple and pink purse. Emily had left without it.

I grabbed it while watching Zoe and her friends talk in the grass. She glanced over at me and winked. I nodded at her before sprinting back to the woods as quickly as my scrawny legs could carry me.

When I hopped through the trees, Wyatt was waiting for me all by himself. The clan was nowhere to be seen.

"Well done," he said as he held his hands out.

I dropped Emily's purse into his palms. "So that's it?"

His mask moved as he spoke. "That's it."

Suddenly Zoe stepped into the woods, joining us. Her faced looked like she had been slapped around by the dirt fairy. It even looked like her lip was bloody. Man, had she gotten into a fight since I last saw her talking to her friends?

"Happy?" she asked.

"Quite," Wyatt answered. His eyes looked piercing from the ninja mask surrounding them. I couldn't wait to get my hands on one! The mask, I mean… not his *eyes*. For the record, I had no intention of getting my hands on one of his eyes.

Wyatt opened the purse and dumped the contents onto the ground. Zoe clenched her fists in anger.

"Why would you do that?" She asked. "Why not just take what you want and leave the rest somewhere she could find it?"

Wyatt chuckled. "Because that's silly. The point of stealing it is that it's ours to do what we want with it."

My cousin stared at the short ninja. I thought time had stopped because of how thick the tension was. I was waiting for her to throw a punch at him. She tended to do things like that when she was angry.

"I'm out," she said, raising her palms. "This is making me feel like throwing up."

"You can't just leave now, sweetheart!" Wyatt sneered. "You're a member of the clan and guilty of theft! If you leave, we'll make sure you regret it!"

The rest of the ninja clan started stepping out from behind the trees. Many of the ninjas were pulling their masks back over their faces. Their eyes looked angry.

"Whatever," Zoe said as she stepped through the trees. From the other side of the foliage, she spoke to me. "You comin' or what?"

I looked at Wyatt who was still holding Emily's

purse. The ninja was calmly staring at me, shaking his head slowly. It was one of the hardest things I've said in my life. "Sorry, Zoe. I think I'll stay here."

Friday. 9:30 AM. Art class.

I got to school late this morning, and it wasn't by accident. All night, my stomach had twisted and turned from not only stealing a girl's purse, but also betraying my own cousin. My parents didn't seem to notice, but my sister sure did. She was nice about it, not by asking what was wrong, but hanging out with me while I wasted time playing video games.

When I woke up, I acted sick. My mom bought it for a little bit, at least enough to skip homeroom. But when she caught me out of bed and playing basketball in my driveway, she took me straight to school. She barely gave me time to get ready! I arrived for second period art class, but with messed up hair.

When I walked into class, I expected Zoe to scold me, but it was worse than that. She completely *ignored* me. I know she saw me walk into the room – everyone did and made fun of my hair. But she just sat at her desk with her watercolors painting unicorns or something.

When I looked at her canvas, I saw that she was painting flowers. I was wrong about the unicorns.

"Hey," I said.

She didn't answer.

"Hey Chase," said Brayden. The desks in the room were separated into clumps of four. He was in the clump behind Zoe's.

"Hi," I said, unenthusiastically.

He switched from his clump of desks to the one Zoe was at. "Did you hear about the food drive money?"

I had only gotten to school so I hadn't heard about *anything* yet. "No. What about it?"

"It's *gone*," Brayden said. "The container is

completely *empty*."

"What are you talking about? That thing was filled with cash and sitting in the front office! Somebody stole it?"

"*Just* the money. The container's still there, and nobody knows who did it," Brayden said.

I felt that same sick feeling roll around in my guts. I had to take a seat and breathe slowly through my nose. I didn't know what it meant, but I had my suspicions. And from the looks of it, Zoe did too.

"Anyway," Brayden continued. "That's that, so you're all caught up in case you see a mountain of cash sitting somewhere."

I watched in silence as he returned to his seat.

"Happy with your new friends?" Zoe asked. She wasn't even trying to hide her sarcasm.

I didn't want to make excuses. "I'm sorry about yesterday. *Really*."

"*Really*?"

"*Really*!"

Zoe tapped the water off her paintbrush and set it on a wet paper towel next to her canvas. "So you quit then, hmm?"

I didn't answer.

"You've quit, and you also returned Emily's purse, right?" Zoe asked. The way she rose her voice grated on me.

"Well, *no*," I whispered.

“Of course not,” Zoe said. “You know how I know? Because she called me last night wondering if I had seen it anywhere. You know what I had to do then?”

I took a breath. I remember it being the longest pause in the history of all pauses. “What?”

She leaned over and whispered. “I *lied* to her.”

That was it. If she was going to give me a guilt trip, I didn’t have to take it. “I didn’t *ask* you to lie! You could’ve told her the truth!”

“That I *helped* you steal it?” she whispered coarsely. “Yeah, right. And commit social suicide? Forever to be branded as a *klepto*?”

“Whatever, Zoe. You *knew* what you were doing.”

I could hear her teeth grinding. “That I was helping my cousin fit in at a school he was new at? That I felt so bad for him because he’s such a *dork* that I couldn’t stand to watch him be *alone*?”

I nodded my head, destroyed by what she said. “*There* it is.”

“There *what* is?”

“The truth. You’ve finally revealed how you really feel about it,” I said, surprised by the shaking in my own voice. “Well you don’t have to worry about it anymore. I guess I’ll leave you alone forever then. Happy?”

Ah, the classic guilt trip. I was good at those. Now I only had to a wait a few seconds for her apology. And in three… two… one…

“*Good*!” she said as she stood from her desk. She stormed up to the art teacher. He handed her a hall pass, and she disappeared out the door.

And there I sat, smug smile on my face, waiting for an apology that wasn't going to be delivered anytime soon.

I'd never felt so stupid in my life.

Friday. 10:35 AM. Gym class.

I wasn't sure what to do in gym. Zoe had already gathered with her group of friends, which included Emily. They stood just outside the girl's locker room, gossiping and talking loudly to one another.

I was on the other side of the gymnasium, standing alone until Brayden joined me.

"Where's Zoe?" he asked.

I nodded my head in her direction.

"Oh," he said. "I heard you guys arguing in art class."

Staring at the floor, I made sure not to make eye contact. The fact that he heard us talking meant he might have heard about Emily's purse. "What did you hear us say?"

"*Everything*," he sighed.

I took a breath and continued studying the

gymnasium floor.

"Kind of shady to steal a girl's purse like that," Brayden said. "Kind of *shadier* to put that pressure on a family member."

I feigned a large smile. "Thaaaaaanks. I'll be sure to remember that next time."

"Told you those were the bad guys," Brayden said.

Would this kid just shut up already? "Look, I'm not arguing with you here. Alright? Would you mind walking away?"

Brayden chuckled as he shook his big dumb head. Finally he pushed himself off the wall and started walking toward the gymnasium doors.

I let everyone filter out before exiting. I didn't feel like having anyone walk behind me.

When I reached the track, I waited until the coast was clear before entering the ninja's secret hideout. Wyatt was already there in full uniform, as were most of the other ninjas. It was strange because they were all lined in a circle. At the center of the circle was a ninja uniform, tightly folded and resting on a small wooden table.

"Welcome, brother," Wyatt's voice said from beneath his mask. "You're one of us now."

I won't lie to you – all the guilt I had felt earlier *disappeared.* The sun was pouring in from overhead, slipping through the leaves of trees. The ground twinkled from specks of water left behind from the morning dew and moist air, like diamonds sprinkled around the hideout. The rays of light fell upon the ninja uniform as if God himself had blessed the cotton it was made from. I scratched at my eyebrow, careful to hide a tear that had formed in the side of my eye.

Wyatt put his arm around me. "There's a spot behind those trees for you to change your clothes. Be quick, brother. We have an important task for you when you're ready."

It was everything I could do to keep from squealing like my sister on Christmas. I did my best to answer calmly, but it only came out in a rapid slur. "*SureI'llberightback!*"

The ninja costume fit like a glove, I tell you. It was like a finely tailored suit that a rich gentlemen would special order from Europe. When I emerged from the tree, many of my ninja brothers and sisters gasped and clapped softly. I made the outfit look *good*. Or scary. It might've been because my overly skinny body made it look like I was the grim reaper. Whatever though – strike fear into my enemies, right?

Another ninja to the left of me whipped out a couple bags of Oreos, and we continued our celebration with cookies. I don't even care how silly that sounds – ninjas and cookies are two of the most *awesome* things on the planet. Of course they'd go great together!

Wyatt sat by my side with a mouthful of cookie. He chewed it sloppily like a dog. "I'm thankful that you've chosen to become a member of my clan."

"Are there other clans?" I asked.

"No," Wyatt said. "Are you ready for the task we've specifically chosen for you?"

I set my Oreos down on the little table. My first job as a ninja, and in a real ninja uniform – *of course* I was ready! "Yes, tell me what I must do."

Wyatt paused. "Are you sure? You wear the uniform now so you can't reject any kind of duty you're given."

For a second, I imagined he said "doodie," and I laughed. "No, I won't reject anything. Whatever you want from me, consider it done."

Wyatt nodded, and made a "tch tch" sound with his cheek. Immediately, one of the other members of the clan tossed a backpack to the ground in front of me. It was bright red with speckled straps.

I studied it for a moment. I had seen a backpack like this before, but where? And then it hit me – I saw the same bag sitting by Zoe's desk earlier in the week. This was *Zoe's* backpack.

"Why do you have that?" I asked.

Wyatt shook his head. "Members of my clan don't ask questions when they're given a task, and yours is simple. All you have to do is take this bag to the front office."

"Sneak it in there? You want me to walk through the school wearing this ninja uniform?"

"No," Wyatt said. "That's why it'll be easy. After gym, you'll change into your normal street clothes and simply take this bag to the front desk. You'll deliver it to the principal, and tell them that you found it under a bush outside."

I looked at Zoe's backpack. Could it have been a coincidence? Could this just be the same bag that she has? As I scanned the side of it, I saw her name scribbled on the plastic shield, complete with the smiley face in the "o." This was definitely her bag.

"What's inside?" I asked.

"Vengeance," Wyatt said.

"Vengeance? For what?"

Wyatt pulled his mask back and revealed his face. A face that was filled with anger. "She *rejected* our offer, and embarrassed me in front of my clan. That *cannot* go unpunished. *Enough* questions. As a member of this clan, you must deliver this bag to the office and say nothing else of it. Do you understand?"

Reluctantly, I nodded.

"Do *not* open this bag, or you will suffer the same fate as your cousin," Wyatt warned.

There was that same sick feeling in my gut. I almost felt like barfing.

Friday. 11:25 AM. Between gym class and lunch.

I waited until everyone in gym had returned to the locker rooms before I stepped out of the woods. The other ninjas had changed clothes and returned with the rest of the class. Mr. Cooper wasn't too attentive so the fact that I wasn't with them slid past him pretty easily.

With Zoe's backpack slung over my shoulder, I started hiking across the track and field. If I went in through the gymnasium doors, I was sure to get caught so I decided to walk around the school to where the front offices were.

The bag was heavy on my back. Heavier than a normal bag should be anyway. I imagined she had all her textbooks in it, but I knew that wasn't the truth. Why would Wyatt call it "vengeance" if I were simply delivering an item to the lost and found?

My stomach curdled once more, and I couldn't take

it. Zoe was my cousin, and even though she hurt my feelings, she was *still* family. I've already betrayed her once, and I didn't want to do it again.

I set the bag on the sidewalk and stared at it. I didn't want to see what was inside, partially because whatever was in there was there because I'm an *idiot*. It's *my* fault that Zoe was in this mess, and I was prepared to do whatever it took to get her out of it.

My hand shook as I gripped the zipper. The cold piece of metal stung from pinching it too tightly. I clenched my jaw and decided to treat the bag like a bandaid – rip it open and get it over quickly.

I jerked my hand into the air, unzipping Zoe's red backpack. The bag lifted off the ground and flipped upside-down. As it landed, hundreds of coins rolled out as lumps of cash fell to the pavement.

"Oh no," I whispered. My knees betrayed me, and I fell to the ground, staring at all the money that spilled from the red bag.

There was a yellow sheet of paper sticking out from under the coins. I could only read part of it, but I knew what it said. When I yanked it free, I found that I was right.

"Student Hunger Drive, Money Donations," was printed in bold black ink on the yellow paper.

The food drive money that was found missing this morning had somehow reached its way into Zoe's backpack. The ninjas had stolen it and were planning on framing her.

This was bad. Not *just* bad, but *epic* bad. Like "*end of the world*" bad. Zoe wouldn't just get a slap on the wrist for something like this – she would get expelled and then it would be on her permanent record. Her parents would ground her for the rest of her life! My parents would never let us hang out together again! She'll probably grow old and die alone because of the contents of this backpack!

I couldn't take it to the office! Not even if I told them the truth because c'mon, a ninja clan in the woods wants to frame a sixth grade girl because she refused to join? I just *lived* through it, and even *I* don't believe that tale!

I scooped the loose change and clumps of paper money back into Zoe's backpack, and then I remembered that Brayden said it was nearly three grand that was stolen. If you've never held three grand in a backpack, let me tell you right now that it's not very light.

Paranoid, I made sure nobody was outside watching me. If Wyatt was able to steal all this money from the front office, he could easily be spying on me right at that moment.

Friday. 11:35 AM. Lunch.

I decided against walking through the front doors of the school for obvious reasons. If *anyone* had stopped to ask what I was doing, I knew I'd buckle and act super suspicious. I guess a backpack with three thousand dollars will do that to ya.

Instead, I walked to the doors of the cafeteria. Coincidentally, they were next to the gym doors so the trek wasn't that far.

The cafeteria was bustling with activity as kids walked to their tables with trays filled with gross food. I could see Zoe at a table with her friends. Emily was right next to her. Brayden was sitting alone at the table nearest the door. Once I snuck in, I immediately dashed to the seat across from him.

He looked up from his tray. "Where's your food?"

I continued to scan the room for Wyatt. "Not so hungry."

Brayden took a bite of his mashed potatoes. "What's with the backpack?"

"Y'know," I said, still keeping an eye out. I couldn't see Wyatt anywhere. "Sometimes I like to just carry my bag around."

With a mouthful of food, Brayden spoke, pointing his fork at the bag. "That's not your bag, dummy. That's Zoe's."

"What?" I asked, shocked. "Did I grab the wrong bag again? How silly of me."

"Shut up," Brayden said with a hint of anger in his voice. "You have it on purpose. What's your deal, Chase?"

I glanced at the werewolf hunter across the table as he took a drink from his milk carton. His eyes were soft and doughy. Could he be trusted? We'll see. "This bag is filled with the money from the food drive."

Brayden spit out his milk, spraying it across the table and my face. He punched at his chest as he coughed out the words, "Are you serious?"

I wiped the milk off my cheeks. "Yes! Keep it down, will ya?"

"*Did you steal that money?*" he leaned over and whispered.

"*No!* But I have it now," I replied. "This is Zoe's bag, and I'm supposed to take it to the office! Wyatt wants to frame her for stealing the money so she'll get in trouble!"

"*'In trouble'* is what she'll *wish* she got in! More than likely, she'll get in "*dead meat*'!"

"I know!" I said. "And I don't know what to do!"

Brayden leaned forward and looked over both his shoulders, I think to make sure no one was listening in on our conversation. "You need to get that cash back into the container in the office."

"Of course that's what I'd *love* to do, but I doubt that it's as easy as walking it in there!" I said loudly. Luckily the students in the cafeteria were louder.

Brayden leaned back in his chair and pried open his milk carton. After taking a sip, he set the drink back down on his tray, and then with a milk mustache, he spoke. "I'll provide the distraction. No worries there. We'll do it after I finish my food."

“I hope you know what you’re doing,” I said, genuinely feeling a glimmer of hope for the first time since I found the money.

He nodded as he finished his meal. Yeah, it was the weirdest thing. He just kept on nodding while eating his food, but was I going to say anything about it? Nope, because he was going to *help* me. Brayden had moved up on the ladder from a person I hardly knew, to a true friend.

Friday. 11:45 AM. In the hallway during lunch.

I followed Brayden as he led the way. He was keeping an eye out for anyone in front of us while I made sure nobody was behind. Zoe's red backpack was getting heavier on my shoulder, and I couldn't wait to get rid of the darn thing.

"It's right around this corner," said Brayden. Good thing too because being the new kid in school, I hardly knew my way around.

"What's the plan?" I asked.

Brayden poked his head around the corner and glanced through the windows of the front office. "Not sure yet."

The front office was separated by a large counter that was as high as my neck. Behind the counter were several desks with adults that stared blankly at their computer monitors. One of the adults was the secretary. I think she stayed in the office the entire day so I'm at sea about how Wyatt ever stole the money in the first place. Like I said before, he must've been *good*.

"There are three people working at their desks," said Brayden. "I think if I make enough noise and run down the hallway, they'll probably chase me."

I shook my head. "That won't work. Only *one* of them will chase after you, if even *that*. More than likely, they'll page the security guard to come after you. We have to think of something else."

And then came a familiar voice from behind us. "You could drop the bag off as I instructed you to."

I could tell it was Wyatt. When I turned around, he was standing there with his arms at his sides, wearing a scowl across his face. Outside of his ninja outfit, he looked like any other short kid in the school. Average. Forgettable.

Behind him were several other students I didn't recognize, but from how they were standing, it was clear that it was the rest of the clan.

"I can't do that," I said as I pulled Zoe's backpack tighter on my shoulders.

"You don't really have a choice, do you?" Wyatt asked with an ugly smirk.

"Oh, but I think I do," I replied. "You see, *I'm* the one with the bag and the money. Not you."

Wyatt chuckled, as did the rest of the clan behind him. "You're only delaying the inevitable. This can go down in two ways – you can dump the bag in the office, telling them what I told you to say, or you can get caught out here with a backpack full of three grand. Pretty sure they won't believe *any* story you tell them about me. After all, I'm just an average Joe at this school. I barely have any friends, right?"

The ninja leader was right. If I choose one path, then *Zoe* gets busted. If I wait too long, a teacher will eventually come along, and then *I'll* get busted. That'd be a great way to start a new school, huh? Get caught stealing money from hungry kids. Either way, *Wyatt* wins.

I had to do something to upset his plan and flip it over on him. I thought frantically about what to do, but couldn't think of anything to save my life. I looked at Brayden, hoping he would have a suggestion, but he only shrugged his shoulders.

"You're running out of time, Chase," Wyatt sneered.

"Chase?" said a girl's voice. When I looked over, I saw Zoe walking with her friends. *Of course* they'd show up at this exact moment. Isn't that my luck?

"Hey, Zoe," I said, staring at the floor.

"Why do you have my backpack?" she asked,

growing visibly upset. "Oh I get it, you were probably instructed to steal *my* stuff too, weren't you?"

Emily spoke up this time. "*Too*? Did your cousin steal my purse?"

I could feel my face getting hotter at the embarrassment. I was about to answer before Zoe spoke again. "Yes, as a matter of fact, he *did*."

"Not without a special someone's help," Wyatt laughed.

Zoe turned around, and did what should've been done right after the incident. "Emily, I'm sorry, but I helped my cousin take your purse during gym class yesterday."

Emily's jaw dropped for a moment in pure shock. The hallway was so quiet that I swear I heard a cricket somewhere, *dying* of quietness. "But why?"

My cousin paused. "Because I was stupid. I thought helping Chase would get him some friends. I mean, *look* at him and how *pathetic* he is!"

"Thanks," I murmured.

Zoe sighed. "Whatever was in your purse, I promise I'll return to you. Honestly, I will. I'm just so sorry that it even happened."

Emily finally closed her mouth and gulped. And then the most awesome thing happened. She smiled. "It's okay. No big deal. That was my *gym class* purse. All I keep in there is a spare stick of deodorant and a couple quarters for a soda after class."

Zoe's face lit up as if a dark shroud was lifted from

it. "I owe you a bunch of quarters then!"

Emily laughed. "Nah, don't worry about it. You did it 'cause you care for your cousin. It was worth it, right?"

I wish I had friends as cool as that.

Wyatt clenched his fists and spoke through his clenched jaw. "It doesn't matter anyway since you're stuck here with a bag fulla money!"

"A bag full of money?" Zoe asked. "Does my backpack have money in it?"

I couldn't answer, but Zoe could read me like a book. "The money from the food drive… it's all in there, isn't it?"

I nodded as Wyatt laughed. His ninja minions laughed along with him, which made the hallway echo with villainous guffawing. If this didn't attract any teachers, I don't know what would.

I did the only thing I could think of. I let the backpack fall into my hands, and whipped it at Wyatt as hard as I could to shut him up. Distracted by his own moment of glory, he didn't see the bag coming, and it hit him straight in the face.

Zoe's bag burst open as loose change and tightly wound balls of cash fell to the floor, amidst the sound of gasping students.

Wyatt let out a loud cry as he tumbled backward into the members of his ninja clan. The students caught him and pushed him back to his feet, whispering quickly among themselves.

And this is the part where things went a little blurry.

Embarrassed, Wyatt threw a punch that landed solidly on my chin. The shock of pain blasted through my body and everything went bright white for a second. The next thing I knew I was on the floor of the hallway, laying in the middle of a circle of shouting kids, yelling something about a fight.

I felt a sharp pain from my lip. As I stood up, I rubbed my fingers across my mouth. Wyatt's punch must've busted my lip open. Blood was all over my fingertips. All I wanted to do was punch him back. Everything inside me boiled with anger and suddenly, the entire world was painted red.

I spit on the floor and saw Zoe's backpack lying next to me. She was also standing in the crowd of shouting students, but she was standing perfectly still. She looked sad.

I glanced back at Wyatt as he landed another punch right into my gut. I immediately felt like puking as I clutched at my stomach. I was the new kid at the school. Scrawny and dorky. And I was getting my butt kicked in front of everyone. Wyatt was going to win the fight no matter how hard I fought back so I did the opposite of what I wanted to do…

I decided to let him win.

Standing again, I looked at him. He was bouncing

around like some kind of karate master with his hands in the air, waving them back and forth in front of his body. I smiled because it looked like he was playing with one of those puppets attached to strings… what are they called? Oh yeah, *marionettes*.

Another punch from Wyatt met with my cheek this time. I saw it coming, but didn't even try to block it. Why bother? Everything was my fault anyhow, so maybe I deserved a proper beating.

And then the crowd started to calm down a little. Wyatt kept dancing and breathing heavily, occasionally letting out a "whaaaaaaaa," the way Bruce Lee did in those old movies. He was so engulfed in the moment that he didn't even realize everyone had stopped cheering.

Suddenly, I realized what was happening. Somehow in this moment, I had become the bigger man. By refusing to fight back, I was taking a stand of my own. I was standing up to a filthy rotten bully. And it gave me strength.

I watched as he threw a kick into the air. Punches are one thing, but getting kicked is a whole other level of "ouch." His foot landed on my arm, scorching pain down my spine. I wasn't sure how much more I could take of this, but I returned to my position in front of him.

"Fight back!" Wyatt yelled. The frustration in his voice was clear.

He swung a right hook at me, but this time I dodged it by leaning backward. "I won't. You're not worth it. If I fight, then *you* win. If I turn this bag into the office, then *you* win. If I get caught with it, then *you* win. The only way for me to stop this is if I refuse to play along with your manipulative games. All I should've done was walk away from the beginning, but I can't do that now, can I? I'm stuck here so the best thing to do is to refuse to fight back."

From the corner of my eye, I could see Zoe smile at me. It was a proud smile.

"Hit me!" Wyatt screamed again as he threw another hook.

I dodged it as I did before.

One of his ninja minions put their hand on his shoulders. "Come on, man. This is getting weird. Let's just get outta here."

Several of the other ninjas agreed.

Wyatt swung around and slapped the kid in the face. "Don't tell me what to do! And don't you *ever* touch me!"

The ninja leader flung back around with his arm swinging wide. It moved too quickly for me to back away from. All I could do was flinch.

But the punch never landed. I pried my eyes open and saw a furious Mr. Cooper dragging Wyatt away from me. The circle of students filled the entire hallway.

"*He* started it!" Wyatt shouted as he kicked his feet. "I caught him with the stolen money! Look at it! It all came pouring out of that red backpack!"

Mr. Cooper released Wyatt's arm and stepped forward, staring at the floor covered in cash.

Everyone in the hallway was silent, which made it easy for Wyatt to keep shouting. "That's Zoe's bag! They were in on it together! They *both* stole the money, and I caught them! When I confronted him, he started fighting me! I *had* to defend myself!"

Mr. Cooper pushed the change around with his foot until he saw the yellow sheet of paper that labeled it the food drive money. He glanced around the hallway of students. By this time, several of the other teachers had joined, trying to push the kids away from the dropped cash.

"Who's responsible for this?" Mr. Cooper asked.

"I already said *they* were!" Wyatt screamed, pointing at my cousin and me.

Mr. Cooper raised his hand to Wyatt, instructing him to be silent. "I didn't ask *you*, I asked *them*," he said gesturing to everyone in the hallway.

There was no way that any of Wyatt's ninja clan would fess up to it, and if they did, who would believe them? Everyone else in the hallway knew nothing of Wyatt's plan so all they were good for was a shoulder to shrug. The backpack was Zoe's, there was no doubt about that, and when they would get around to asking why it was in *her* bag, she would claim it was stolen. I doubt she would say anything about the ninjas, but even if she did, who in the world would believe her?

I looked at my cousin. She had a worried look on her face as she glanced back. It looked like there were tears forming in her eyes. She was family, but more *importantly*, she was a *friend.*

When Zoe was questioned about Emily's stolen purse, she immediately admitted her fowl up. I took that as a lesson in integrity.

I nodded at Zoe, and then I spoke. "*I* took the money."

Strangely, it was the ninja clan that gasped loudest.

"I *told* you!" Wyatt said, slapping his hands together.

"No, *I* took the money," Brayden suddenly shouted as he stepped forward.

Wait, what? Why did Brayden just say that?

"No! *I* took it!" Zoe shouted.

And then another weird thing happened – other students started stepping forward, confessing that they stole the food drive money.

"*I* did it," said a short girl with red hair. She was cute, but that's beside the point.

"It was *me*," said one of the taller students.

"*I* took the money," said yet another.

I watched as several of the ninjas stepped forward and did the same. I can't imagine Wyatt was too happy that they were doing it.

Wyatt's face grew bright red as he clenched his fists again. "*They* took the money!" he screamed as he jumped at me.

Mr. Cooper caught him by his collar and pulled him back instantly. The coach pushed the ninja leader into the doorway of the front office, and then turned around. "I don't know *who* did this, but at this point it's clear that Wyatt had *something* to do with it. At the moment, the money is returned, which is more important than *who* took it. I think most of us are just thankful that it's back. Everyone clear out of the hallway so we can gather up the cash and put it back where it belongs. But mark my words that this *isn't* over. We'll find out who did it eventually, so it would be best if the guilty party stepped forward at a later time, in *private*," the coach said as he slammed the office door shut.

"Wow," said Zoe as she looked at my face. "You got your butt *kicked*!"

"Yeah," I said. "Seems like I might be good at that, huh? Maybe I can start a club or something."

Emily pulled a tissue from one of her other purses. Maybe it was her "lunchtime" purse or something. "I think it's manly," she said as she started dabbing my bloody lip with the tissue. Her eyes were cute.

"Sick," said Brayden. "Get a room."

I laughed, but had to hold my side from the pain.

"Chase," said a student from behind. It was one of the members of the ninja clan. "That was the most awesome thing any of us had ever seen in our entire lives. It takes a boy to start a fight, but it takes a man to end one. You ended it with so much honor that my face wants to *melt* off!"

"Cute picture you paint," said Zoe.

The boy continued. "We are without a leader now."

"What about Wyatt?" I asked.

"He's a coward that just wants to control people

and show how strong he is," said the boy. "We need a clan leader like you. Brave. Honorable. Able to stand up to bullies. Not beat them down."

I nodded. Ninjas were cool, but this whole thing turned out to be more of a pain than it might've been worth. I smiled with blood on my teeth. "I'll think about it. How's that sound?"

"We'll need to know soon. There are rumors of a pirate invasion in the near future," The boy bowed as did the rest of the clan before turning and walking away.

A *pirate* invasion? What kind of insane school *was* this?

"Looks like you might have some friends after all?" Zoe laughed.

"Maybe," I said. "That's if I don't get expelled."

"Nobody knows who took the money, and I doubt the teachers here will make any fuss about it," said Brayden. "As long as it's back, they're happy."

Mr. Cooper opened the door to the office and leaned his head out. He pointed at me and said, "Chase, come in here for a moment please."

"Am I in trouble?" I asked as I wiped my lip clean with Emily's tissue.

Mr. Cooper shook his head. "No, it's just that you're a bloody mess. The nurse should have a look at you to make sure you're alright."

I paused as I glanced at Zoe and my friends. I didn't want to be lured into the office just to be told I wasn't welcome at the school anymore, but understood that it might be happening.

"Look, Wyatt already admitted to the whole thing being his fault. He broke down the second I shut this door," Mr. Cooper laughed. "It really *is* because you're bleeding all over the carpet. What if a parent walked in at this second and saw your battered face?"

"I could probably win a dinosaur sized lawsuit," I replied.

Zoe laughed. Brayden didn't. Maybe he didn't get it.

Mr. Cooper knocked on the wood of the door. "Just get in here."

I walked to the office door and pushed it open. I could see the top of Wyatt's head over the front counter. He was sitting in the principal's office, probably waiting for his parents. How funny. A ninja getting scolded by his parents.

I turned around and took one last look at Zoe. She nodded at me once, and I returned the gesture. Pushing the door fully open, I stepped into the front office and let it shut behind me.

Buchanan School was a strange place, and though it was new and scary, I'm not sure I'd have it any other way. Beside, I think there's a ninja clan that needs a leader.

My name is Chase Cooper, and I'm a ninja.

Stories – what an incredible way to open one's mind to a fantastic world of adventure. It's my hope that this story has inspired you in some way, lighting a fire that maybe you didn't know you had. Keep that flame burning no matter what. It represents your sense of adventure and creativity, and that's something nobody can take from you. Thanks for reading! If you enjoyed this book, I ask that you help spread the word by sharing it or leaving an honest review!

- Marcus

m@MarcusEmerson.com

AND DON'T MISS THIS
LAUGH-OUT-LOUD MYSTERY!

NOW AVAILABLE!

TURN THE PAGE FOR A SNEAK PEEK!

My head was spinning, and I had no idea where I was. All I knew for sure was that I was sitting on a chair in a dark room. It was cold, and I could hear water dripping from somewhere behind me. Plus my socks were wet.

Wonderful… I *hate* wet socks.

"Hello?" I tried saying out loud, but my mouth was as dry as uncooked pasta so it only came out as, "*Bleh-bloh?*"

From the shadows across the room, I heard a wooden chair plunk on the floor. "Welcome back, Mr.

Brody Valentine," said a boy's voice. "Funny last name you have, isn't it?"

I took a breath and blinked. "There are some things in life we can't choose. Last names… would be one of those things."

"You're right," he replied, stepping forward, but staying hidden in the shadows. "Some of us are just born unlucky, aren't we?"

I remained silent, studying the room while the kid kept talking. From the look of it, I figured I was in a larger storage closet, probably near the school's cafeteria. The smell of steamed broccoli lingered in the air. You'd think that would be proof enough that I was around the lunchroom, but the boy's locker room *also* smelled like steamed broccoli. I *know*, right? *So* nasty.

The boy continued. "When you woke up this morning, you had no idea of the little adventure that awaited you at school, did you?"

I cracked a smile and chuckled softly.

"Unless," the boy whispered, "you *did* know of this adventure, which would mean you're just as guilty as the *rest* of them. Tell me, Brody, *where's* the journal?"

"Someplace safe," I replied as I sat up in my chair. My head was swelling with pain. "Someplace far away from here."

The boy paused. "You know this is over, right? This little game you and your friends are playing… they've already ratted you out. You're *done.*"

I wasn't sure if the boy was bluffing or not so I

didn't respond. I don't think anyone would've tattled on me, but after the day I've had, I couldn't really be sure. I knew that sixth grade was going to be tough, but not *this* tough. Secret agent stuff, spy gear, special codes, and conspiracies – that was a lot for *anyone* to carry on their shoulders, especially someone like me!

I'm literally a nobody at Buchanan School, or at least, I *used* to be before today. Now it's almost like I'm the most wanted kid in the entire school, and trust me when I say it *wasn't* on purpose.

My name is Brody Valentine and this is the story of how I accidentally became a secret agent. Don't make fun of my last name either. Like I said earlier… there are some things in life we *can't* choose.

I remember it like it was just this morning… probably because it *was* just this morning…

Check it out – that's my school picture. Scrawny

little dweeb, right? Hardly secret agent material. I bet spy agencies have this photo hanging in their offices to show them what kind of person *not* to hire. My parents tell me I have a big heart and that's all that matters, but telling that to a sixth grade boy is the same thing as beating a video game on easy – it's something that takes almost no effort, but at least you can move on to the next game.

I know. I get it. I'm not destined to be a great football player or ultimate fighter, but I accept that. Instead, I'll be the super billionaire computer nerd that controls half of the world and—wait, that makes me sound like an evil villain, but I'm not *that* either.

I'm just an ordinary dude, at a *not* ordinary school called Buchanan. It's important to note that my school is trying this new thing where the sixth graders have the freedom to choose their own classes like they would in middle school. It's a neat idea, but it doesn't make middle school *less* of an adjustment. It just makes sixth grade that much *more* of an adjustment.

I got to Buchanan a few minutes before homeroom. The bus driver always cuts it way too close. Apparently the last stop on his route is a gas station where he gets coffee and donuts for himself. The rest of the students wait in the bus as he sips hot coffee and flirts with the cashier for several minutes. She's *cute*, but seriously? How he still has a job is a mystery to me.

I'm the kid that rushes through the hallways, trying my best not to bump into anyone. You'd only see me if I bonked into you. I usually mumble an apology and keep on going, hoping you don't say anything. Kids would shrug me off as antisocial, but the truth is that I'm just *really* shy.

I was at my locker, placing some books into my backpack. The bell was going to ring in just a few minutes so everyone was rushing through the hallways, doing what they could to be on time.

As I lifted one of my textbooks, I felt a dull ache in my side. Groaning, I dropped the book and stretched my arms back. There was a bruise around my ribcage from gym class the day before. There's a game a few of us play called "Chicken." We're a little too old for the playground at recess, but that doesn't stop us from going over to the monkey bars during gym for this game.

Have you ever played it?

Two people hang from the bars and only use their legs to knock the other person off. Kicking is against the rules, but wrapping your legs around the other person's body isn't. When one kid has a good grip on the other, they try to pull them off the bars. It's not usually dangerous because everyone lands on their feet, but the last time I played I just happened to slip and fall into one of the giant garbage barrels next to the monkey bars, which is how I got the bruise. It was entirely my fault so there weren't any hard feelings.

Over the sound of frantic students, I could hear the morning announcements playing over the speaker system. Large flat screen televisions hung at the end of each hallway and would play an animation of the announcements. Every now and then, it would play a video about keeping the school clean.

A couple weeks ago, someone pulled a prank and hijacked the system, playing a video of a tap dancing cat over and over again. I suspect the televisions are hooked up to a video player somewhere in the building. How else would it be so easy for a dancing cat to get on TV?

As I shut my locker, I heard some students talking nearby.

"Hey," said a boy. "You got any more of that candy?"

"A little bit," a girl replied. "But go get your own! I spent *all* my lunch money on this!"

"But I can't go down there! I still owe them money for the last few candy bars they gave me!" the boy said.

She chuckled at him. "Then I guess you're outta luck. Looks like you'll have to buy some carrots from the *vending* machines."

The boy sighed. "*Sick...*"

I stood at my locker, staring at the two kids having the conversation.

When the girl noticed me, she looked embarrassed, but it quickly turned to anger. "What are *you* lookin' at?"

I wanted to say something sarcastic like, "A new alien life form!" but instead, I went with something safer by *actually* saying, "Nothing, sorry."

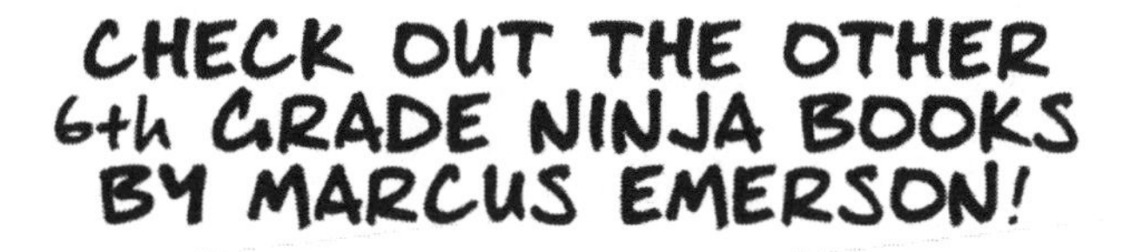
CHECK OUT THE OTHER
6th GRADE NINJA BOOKS
BY MARCUS EMERSON!

diary of a 6th grade ninja 2
pirate invasion
MARCUS EMERSON
diary of a 6th grade ninja 3
rise of the red ninjas
diary of a 6th grade ninja 4
a game of chase
MARCUS EMERSON
diary of a 6th grade ninja 5
terror at the talent show
MARCUS EMERSON
diary of a 6th grade ninja 6
buchanan bandits!
MARCUS EMERSON

Marcus Emerson is the author of several highly imaginative children's books including the 6th Grade Ninja series, and the Secret Agent 6th Grader series. His goal is to create children's books that are engaging, funny, and inspirational for kids of all ages - even the adults who secretly never grew up.

Marcus Emerson is currently having the time of his life with his beautiful wife and their four amazing children. He still dreams of becoming an astronaut someday and walking on Mars.

32248887R00066

Made in the USA
San Bernardino, CA
31 March 2016